TIARA'S HAT PARADE

Kelly Starling Lyons

illustrated by
Nicole Tadgell

Albert Whitman & Company
Chicago, Illinois

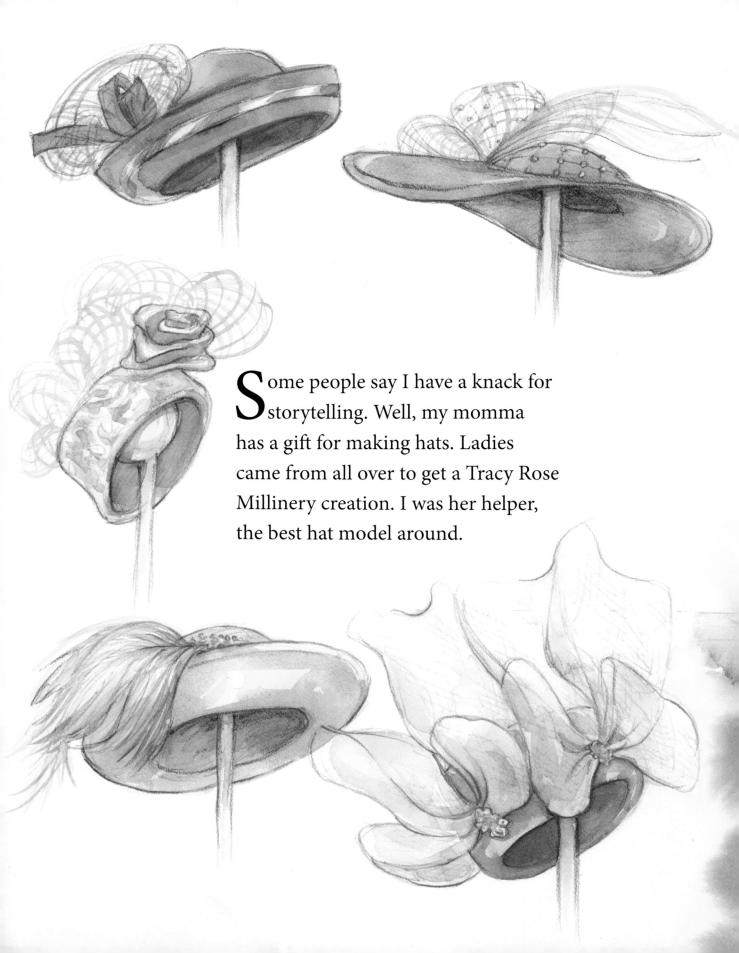

Some people say I have a knack for storytelling. Well, my momma has a gift for making hats. Ladies came from all over to get a Tracy Rose Millinery creation. I was her helper, the best hat model around.

"Hold your head high, Tiara," Momma would say as she slid her Sunny-Day Special on my head. Tangerine with gold feathers fanning out, I felt like a bird showing off its colors. "Now strut. That's right, baby. Show them how it's done."

I would sashay around her studio, and the ladies would clap and shout, "Go on, girl." Their laughter jingled like silver charms.

But when that new store opened with hats that cost way less than Momma's, the stream of ladies slowed to a drip. I waited in the living room window with a smile ready to dazzle. Day after day, nobody came at all.

"We can't eat dreams," Momma said one afternoon, sighing. "That store can afford to sell hats cheaper than I can."

Daddy and I helped Momma pack away her fabric, feathers, beads, sequins, ribbons, and buttons. Then came the hardest part—tucking her hats into boxes. Daddy hugged Momma.

"I can work extra hours," he said. "Don't worry. We'll be okay."

That day, Momma closed her studio for good. Now, no one goes into that room. It just sits at the back of our house quiet and lonely.

When my school had a job opening, Momma went back to
what she did before—teaching art.

"Can we make a new hat after school?" I asked one morning.

"You have homework," she said. "I have work to do too."

"But you're always too busy."

"Let's talk about something else," she said, her voice sharp as a hatpin. Then it was hushed as a feather. "Something happy."

Every day as I walked through the house, I passed her studio. One Saturday when she was out and Daddy wasn't looking, I gently opened the door. It groaned softly like someone slowly waking from a nap.

And I was in.

I saw Momma's hatstands, silent as soldiers standing guard.
I reached for a hatbox and trembled as I raised the lid.
Inside was Momma's Purple Pride. I slid it on and felt a smile
rise up in my heart.

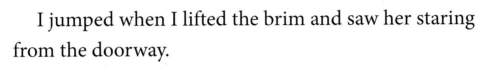

I jumped when I lifted the brim and saw her staring from the doorway.

"This was something special," she whispered.

"Can it be again?" I asked.

"Not now, sweetie," Momma said. "Just put that hat away and come on out. I told you stay out of here."

I held back tears but did as Momma said, tucking the Purple Pride back into its bed. She put her arm around my shoulder. Then she locked the door behind us.

But the next day at recess, I thought about Momma's hats. I pictured them as we drove home. At dinnertime, I slipped in a silent prayer after grace.

"Amen. And please help Momma make hats again."

On Fun Friday at school, Momma let us choose our
art project. My hand shot up.

"Hats," I said.

She cut her eyes at me.

"Please, Mrs. Rose," everyone sang.

Her frown turned to a smile.

"Okay, okay, hats it is."

We made hats with tall crowns and big brims, plain
ones and fancy ones. Momma swept across the room like
a magician, helping us add decorations with waves of her
hand. My friend Matti put on her hat and frowned.

"It's just not right," she said, huffing.

Momma cocked the hat to the side and held up a mirror.
"How about now?" she asked.

"Tea party time," Matti said. Her giggle reminded me of
laughter spilling out of Momma's studio.

I sat up straight and smiled. I knew what to do.

I told Daddy my plan.

"That's a real good idea, Baby Girl," he said, smiling.

We checked with the principal. Daddy got the addresses.

And I got busy. *Come to the Hat Parade at Height Elementary*, I wrote in big colorful letters. *Bring your favorite Tracy Rose hat and a story.*

On the big day, Momma sat in the auditorium
for what she thought was an evening concert. My
classmates and I marched up to the stage wearing our
creations. Then came the hat ladies. They winked at
Momma and paraded to the front.

Mrs. Irving pranced to the microphone first, wearing the scarlet Sass-and-Class with its glittering black swoosh.

"You made this for me to wear to the opening of the Ebony Fashion Fair exhibit. I looked sharp—and I knew it."

Ms. Ball strutted up next wearing the emerald I'm-Telling-You.

"When I wore this to Women's Day, everyone wanted to know where I got it."

"Remember this?" Ms. Coleman twirled in Momma's silver Show Stopper. "I was so nervous when I won that big award. You said, 'With this on, jitters don't stand a chance.'"

One after another, they shared stories. Then I stepped up and pulled out what I made. "This is for you, Momma—the Better Days Bonnet. You made the sun shine with your hats. Maybe this will do the same for you."

I laid it on her head like a crown. Momma's eyes gleamed like morning dew.

"That's all right," the hat ladies shouted.

By the time we left, Momma had a few orders. I could already picture us back in her studio. Funny thing was I didn't just see me modeling hats anymore. I saw me making them too. Momma touched her hat and smiled.

"You got me good," she said, her laughter like jingling charms. "I think you're right, Tiara. Better days are coming."

Author's Note

Some people let hats wear them. But others—they can wear a hat. When you see them coming, you marvel at their class, individuality, and style. For generations of Black women, hats have been a way of being seen. Hats demand respect; they frame our beauty, flair, and grace, which are often overlooked in mainstream media. As the title of Michael Cunningham and Craig Marberry's beautiful coffee table book honoring the tradition attests, our hats are crowns.

Our hats don't just sit there either. They whisper and shout, say *amen*, sing, and rap. Whether worn as an accent for a special occasion or cocked to the side with sass, hats are part of Black women's—and men's—style.

At many churches, hats are a staple. As a kid, I remember checking out the hats of church elders. Floppy, sculpted, majestic, they made the women who wore them stand out. When my mom and grandma took me to fashion shows, I oohed and ahhed at fancy hats trimmed with beads, sequins, and feathers. I admired the hats I saw on music videos—kente cloth, leather, wool, felt—they oozed swag in all different styles.

I found my first hat, as a teen, on a family trip to Washington, DC. Trying on a black hat with a wide brim made me feel powerful. My mom treated me to that one and a red one with a black band. Even when I didn't say a word, those hats spoke for me.

When I grew up and became a mom myself, my daughter and I wore hats to tea parties. We made them for fun. My daughter's eyes sparkled as she added special touches and left her mark on each hat.

As I've learned about hatmakers, or milliners, over the years, I've become a fan of their artistry and talent. They make me think about how important it is to keep the hatmaking tradition alive. I wrote this story as a tribute to Black women milliners—like my aunt Anna, who studied hat design, and Ms. Betty, who has a lovely hat shop in Eden, North Carolina—and the children they dazzle and inspire to follow their path.

Famous Black Milliners

Mae Reeves

In the National Museum of African American History and Culture in Washington, DC, you can visit a gorgeous exhibit that celebrates a millinery shop owned by trailblazing African American businesswoman Mae Reeves. Turban and pillbox styles, hats blooming with flowers, feathers, or tulle—Mrs. Reeves could make them all. Though she had famous customers like Lena Horne and Ella Fitzgerald, customers at the Philadelphia hat shop she opened in the 1940s ranged from wealthy to working-class women. Mae's Millinery Shop became not just a place to buy a piece of glamour but a social forum that even encouraged women to vote.

Mildred Blount

Drawn to hatmaking in her childhood, Mildred Blount applied for a job as an apprentice with John-Frederics, a prestigious millinery. As the first Black woman to work there, her talent shined when she made a miniature historical hat exhibit for the 1939 New York World's Fair. Blount also helped design the hats in the movie *Gone with the Wind*, though at the time, she didn't receive credit. Later in life, she opened her own hat shop with clients that included the famous singer Marian Anderson and the actress and dancer Ginger Rogers. Blount's hats are displayed in several museums.

Vanilla Beane

A milliner for decades, Vanilla Beane has won national accolades for her stylish toppers. In Washington, DC, she worked for a downtown millinery supply shop before opening her own hat shop in 1979. Like the diverse people who were her customers, Mrs. Beane's hats showed different personalities and styles. One of her most famous clients was Dr. Dorothy I. Height, who was president of the National Council of Negro Women for more than four decades and the tenth national president of Delta Sigma Theta Sorority, Inc., whose hats became her trademark. Some of Mrs. Beane's hats are in the collection of the National Museum of African American History and Culture.

For my children, who love to rock hats.
For my mom, who bought me my first one.
And for Aunt Anna, Ms. Betty, and the generations
of Black milliners whose hats dazzle and inspire.
KSL

For YOU! Be creative, be generous, be empathetic.
Rock your day, every day.
NT

Library of Congress Cataloging-in-Publication data is on file with the publisher.

Text copyright © 2020 by Kelly Starling Lyons
Illustrations copyright © 2020 by Nicole Tadgell
First published in the United States of America in 2020 by Albert Whitman & Company
ISBN 978-0-8075-7945-9 (hardcover)
ISBN 978-0-8075-7948-0 (e-book)

Printed in China
10 9 8 7 6 5 4 3 2 1 HH 24 23 22 21 20 19

Design by Rick DeMonico

For more information about Albert Whitman & Company,
visit our website at www.albertwhitman.com.